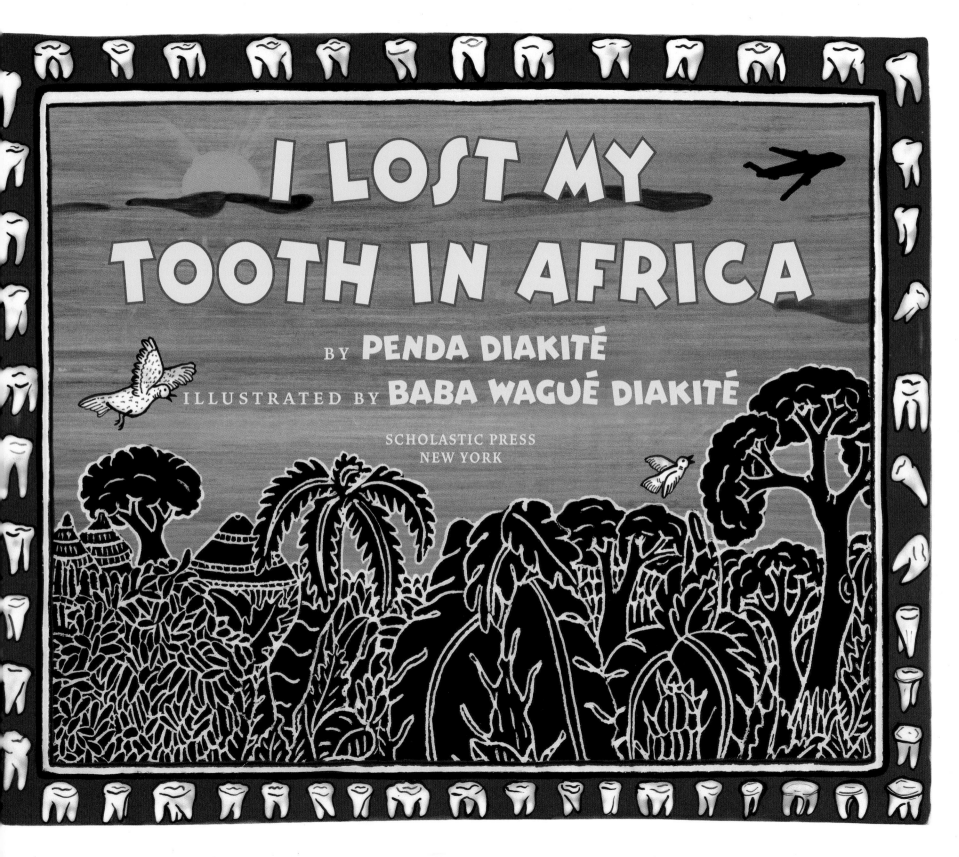

I LOST MY TOOTH IN AFRICA

BY **PENDA DIAKITÉ**

ILLUSTRATED BY **BABA WAGUÉ DIAKITÉ**

SCHOLASTIC PRESS
NEW YORK

A special thank you to Dr. Karl Neuenschwander,
who cares for all of our teeth!

—P. J. D. & B. W. D.

Text copyright © 2006 by Penda Diakité

Illustrations copyright © 2006 by Baba Wagué Diakité

Library of Congress Cataloging-in-Publication Data

Diakité, Penda.

I lost my tooth in Africa / by Penda Diakité ; illustrated by Baba Wagué Diakité.— 1st ed.   p.   cm.

Summary: While visiting her father's family in Mali, a young girl loses a tooth, places it under a calabash, and receives a hen and a rooster from the African Tooth Fairy.

ISBN 0-439-66226-5 (alk. paper)

[1. Family life—Mali—Fiction. 2. Chickens—Fiction. 3. Teeth—Fiction. 4. Mali—Fiction. 5. Africa—Fiction.] I. Diakité, Baba Wagué, ill. II. Title.

PZ7.D54153Iae 2005   [E]—dc22   2004001933

10 9 8 7 6 5 4 3 2 1   06 07 08 09 10

Printed in Singapore 46   First edition, January 2006

The text type was set in 18-point Vendetta medium. The illustrations were created in ceramic tile. Book design by Kristina Albertson

To my African family and to my little sister,
Amina, who was the inspiration for this story
—P. J. D.

To my wife, Ronna Neuenschwander
—B. W. D.

HI! MY NAME IS AMINA.

I live in Portland, Oregon. Today, we are flying to Africa to visit my father's family in Bamako, Mali. Africa is very far from our home in Portland. It takes two days, three planes, and three different continents to get there. Right before landing in Mali, I discover I have a wiggly tooth!

My dad says if you lose a tooth in Africa and put it under a gourd, you will get a chicken from the African Tooth Fairy! I really want to lose my tooth in Africa. So I try tricks with my tongue to help it come out faster.

But nothing happens.

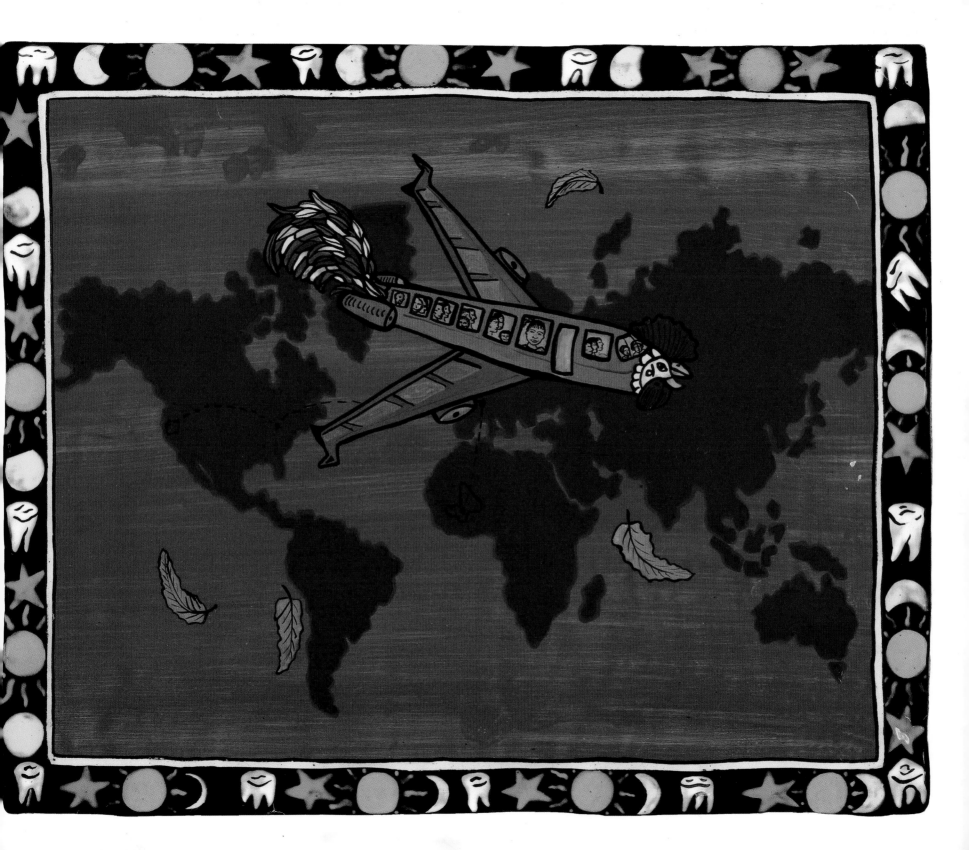

When we arrive, my aunts, uncles, and cousins are here to greet us. They all live together in one compound with N'na, my grandma.

It's very hot here, and the ground is a beautiful sandy orange. Outside our compound there are donkeys, goats, and lots of chickens. The rooster never stops crowing. I wiggle and wiggle my tooth. I can't wait to have my own chicken!

Aunt Kadja has made my favorite dinner. It's rice and onion sauce with African eggplant and tiny noodles. We all eat together around one big bowl. Everyone eats with their right hand. Sometimes, if you're lucky, you get a piece of meat! When I eat, I can feel my tooth moving, but it refuses to come out.

By evening, the world begins to quiet down. The family is home, and neighbors come by to greet us. The stars shine brightly, and the moon glows like a streetlamp. Friends sit in groups in the courtyard, playing games, telling stories, and braiding hair. Sometimes, Grandma N'na sings songs.

As the sky darkens, I climb into my bamboo bed. And after a few stories from my dad, I drift off to sleep. I hope my tooth doesn't fall out at night!

With the first golden rays of the sun, the noisy rooster begins to crow.

"**KAY KAY RAY KAY!**... It's time to get up!"

The first thing we do every morning in Africa is greet Grandma N'na and receive blessings from her. She takes my hand and holds it gently as she begins a long list of benedictions. "May you rise high with strength and knowledge."

"*Amiin,*" I respond after each one.

After breakfast, I run outside to brush my teeth at the papaya tree. That way I can water the tree as I brush!

Suddenly, there is a funny feeling in my mouth. My tongue instantly finds a gap where a tooth had been. I hope I haven't swallowed it. Where is my tooth? I look down. It's on the ground!

I pick it up and run to show my parents. My mom is surprised. My dad helps me place it under a calabash gourd behind the bedroom window. I am so proud. I lost my tooth in Africa! A shiny white tooth! Soon, I will have a chicken of my very own.

All morning I play *tègèrè tillon* with my
cousins, waiting for a chicken to come.
But nothing happens.

    We eat lunch and take a short nap.
Still no chicken.

    We take a walk by the little creek to
check the gardens. Bananas are turning
ripe and the *manioc* is growing tall. We huddle
together to watch a busy weaver bird building its hanging nest
in a palm tree. When we get home, it's already time to take our bucket
baths. The day is almost finished. But no chicken has come.

    Finally, I go to take back my tooth. I feel sad. Maybe the African
Tooth Fairy has forgotten.

But right as I turn over the calabash, two chickens pop out!
One rooster and one hen.
   I am so happy I call to my mom and dad. They are very excited.
   Dad says, "The rooster is more black than white."
   Mom says, "The hen is more white than black."

Right away, I take care of my chickens. I feed them and give them water. My mom and dad help me build a little house for them under the stairway that leads to Grandma N'na's roof. We make adobe bricks and stack them on top of one another. Then we find an old sheet of tin to use as a roof.

Early one morning, I open my chicken coop. There! I see them. White oval eggs in the nest on the dirt floor.

I shout, "**SHAY KEELEEW! SHAY KEELEEW!** Eggs! Eggs!"

Uncle Modibo says that means that chicks will hatch in twenty-one days! I wonder if I will see them before I leave.

When I help Aunt Sali with the meals, the chickens always cluster around my feet. I sneak a handful of millet and rice for them. I like to peel the vegetables because I can feed the peelings to my chickens. When I finish with the vegetables, I smoosh tomatoes with my hands for a good-tasting sauce, and cut squash and cabbage into big quarters so Aunt Sali can boil them.

Later that day, my hen has laid more eggs. That makes me smile, because I know my chickens are happy in our home.

One evening, the hen is squawking. I run outside. The pheasant is trying to steal her eggs! I shoo it away. That pheasant is very crafty and VERY fast. I'll have to watch her carefully.

When I go to sleep that night, I dream about little chicks hatching. I'm getting excited to see what they will look like.

Finally one morning, my dad tells me it is
our last day in Africa. We have to go back to America.
I slowly say good-bye to the things I will miss.
   "**KAWN-BAY**," I say to the mango tree.
   "**KAWN-BAY**," I say to the little creek.
   "**KAWN-BAY**," I say to Africa.

When the time comes to leave, I am sad. I say
good-bye to my African family and friends. Slowly
I walk to the chicken coop to say good-bye to my
chickens.

Then I see it. An egg is hatching! A tiny, wet chick peeks out from a white egg.

"**SHAY DEN! SHAY DEN!**" I shout.

"Chicks! Chicks!"

Everyone comes to see. They all congratulate me.

Just then, another egg hatches.
I am very happy. But I'm very
sad, too. I don't want to leave
my chickens behind.

"Don't worry, Amina," says
Uncle Madou, "I'll take good
care of them. When you come
back, your chicks will be old
enough to lay eggs for you."

I smile so big you can see the empty space where my tooth is missing.
And right away I begin to count the days until we will come back to Africa.

AUTHOR'S NOTE

I was born in Portland, Oregon, in 1992, and I visit my second home in Bamako, Mali, as often as I can. I originally wrote this story when I was eight years old. It's a true story about what happened when my little sister lost her tooth in Africa. I live in Portland with my family, three chickens, one rat, and a parakeet named Murray.

　　　　—PENDA DIAKITÉ

This is my sister Amina holding the chicken she got when she lost her tooth in Africa.

ARTIST'S NOTE

I was born in Mali, West Africa, and now live in Portland, Oregon. I spent much of my childhood in the village, tending herds of sheep and goats. In the evening, we would listen to stories told by our elders. To me, these stories were the true experience of our elders before our time. Later, when I would find myself in the grassland with my herds, I would see these stories springing to life before me. Rabbit is cautious and clever. Hyena is dull and cowardly. Monkey is creative and mischievous. The birds forecast warnings and upcoming events. And the tree is always there in its quiet wisdom, telling me of seasons and cradling me in its strong arms.

There is a proverb from Mali that says, "Raising a child is like planting a tree. When it is tended well, you will enjoy its shade." This has been a great reward for me to illustrate my daughter's book. I have always tried to teach my daughters about my culture in which storytelling is a true way of learning. As the tradition says, "Words must go from old mouths to new ears." Storytelling is a gift to me from my elders and I simply wanted to pass this gift along to my children.

　　　　—BABA WAGUÉ DIAKITÉ

GLOSSARY

There are many different languages spoken in Mali. The national language is Bambara. Most people there speak Bambara as well as their first language. Many people also speak French (the official or government language), because Mali was a colony of France for nearly one hundred years. In our compound, some of our family members speak Bambara, Wassolonga-kan, Sarakole, Songhai, Arabic, French, and a little English. My sister Amina and I speak Bambara when we are in Mali.

Amiin (ah-MEEN) "amen" in Bambara and Arabic.

Amina (ah-MEEN-ah) typical girl's name in West Africa and the Middle East.

Kawn-bay (KAWN-bay) "good-bye" in Bambara.

Manioc (MAN-ee-ahk) French name for cassava, a plant grown in the tropics for its edible rootstocks.

N'na (N-nah) "mother" in Mandinka. In this instance, everyone calls my grandmother N'na out of respect. In Mali, it is only polite to call an elder by an honorable title.

Penda (PEN-dah) "love" in Swahili (Although Swahili is an East African language, my grandmother's given name was Penda, and I was named after her).

Shay den (shay DEN) "chicks" in Bambara (Literally: chicken children).

Shay keeleew (shay kee-LEEW) chicken eggs in Bambara.

Tègèrè tillon (tay-gay-RAY tee-LONE) a Bambara name for a game which involves singing and clapping, where children take turns dancing in the center of a circle.

GRANDMA N'NA'S GOOD NIGHT SONG

Kawn shi day,
Kawn shi day demisenw.
Kawn shi day,
Demisenw ka kanu
Koni ye don ko don ko ye.
(BAMBARA LANGUAGE)

Sweet dreams to all,
Sweet dreams to all children.
Sweet dreams to all,
We care for our children
As sure as there is night and day.

RECIPE

AUNT KADJA'S DJABA DJI (DJA-ba DGEE)
(*African Onion Sauce*)

MAKE SURE YOU HAVE A GROWN-UP HELP YOU!

Peanut oil for sautéing onions and meat

1 cut-up chicken, or stew beef (optional)

6–10 medium onions, sliced

5 cloves of garlic, peeled

1 tsp. dried onion

1 tsp. curry

1 tsp. salt

½ tsp. black pepper

2 thumb-sized pieces of fresh gingerroot, grated

3 tbsp. tomato paste

2 cups chicken broth

2 cups water

½ head of cabbage, cut into 2 pieces

5 small potatoes, peeled and quartered

1 medium eggplant, cut into 8 pieces

1 cup green beans

3 medium carrots, halved

1 cup of the tiniest noodles you can find

4 cups uncooked rice

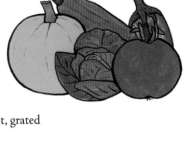

Heat oil. Sauté meat (if you are using meat), then onions. Crush garlic in a garlic press, then add along with dried onion, curry, salt, and pepper. Add grated ginger, tomato paste, and stir. Reduce flame and close lid for 3–10 minutes, until meat and onions are covered with a thick paste. Pour in 2 cups of chicken broth and 2 cups of water, add potatoes, and bring to a boil. Turn down heat and simmer with the lid off for at least 5–10 minutes, mixing from time to time. Then add vegetables and uncooked noodles and simmer 15–20 minutes, until the vegetables have softened. Taste and add salt, if needed. Pour over cooked long grain rice. This will taste even better the second day! Feeds a family of 6.